A Daughter's Christmas Hope

By: Lana Nolan

Contents

Chapter One

For many days Miss Julia Robson walked around in an excited state of hoping for the best and waiting for her mother's health to return. She thought of all the activities she and her mother could partake in again since she had fallen ill months ago. However in the moments before she laid down to slumber, her days seemed as dark as her nights even through fervent prayers for renewed life and vitality for her ailing mother.

Her father, Mr. Giles Robson, took Julia on a daily carriage ride to gather potent remedies from the local town healer, but they were losing their powers to help Mrs. Nell Robson. He was grateful to hear of Doctor Graham Clark passing through on his way home to London. He had spent time traveling throughout the countryside helping those who could not make it to the city for medical help.

This daily drive commanded the selection of food fitting to serve a helpful doctor visiting their home for the first time. Mr. Robson took pride in presenting a good impression and his nerves were beginning to show as the time drew nearer. They arrived back at their home to wait for the doctor but he did not show at the agreed-upon hour. Julia and her father gave each other a sullen look as minutes continued to tick on hour after hour.

She stood and paced back and forth in the sitting room, stopping for a moment to peer out of the window to look for the detained doctor. She saw nothing but the empty brown dirt road leading to their small cottage.

After Julia decided to take a seat on the sofa, she heard the wheels of a carriage roll up outside of the home as her father jumped out of his chair. He ran to open the door to wait for the doctor to make his appearance balancing his weight from one foot to the other. After a few moments, a man walked in to shake hands with her father. Julia rose from the sofa waiting to be greeted. A tall gallant gentleman, well-dressed carrying a black bag followed Mr. Robson into the quaint, sitting room to greet Julia, his eyes fixated on her welcoming smile.

"We have been awaiting your arrival," her father said.

Mr. Robson welcomed him into their home to help save her mother from the painful coughing coming from the bedroom. He paid no attention to their meager dwelling insisting to see his new patient in the room in the back of the house. Mr. Robson rushed past Julia leading the doctor to his wife as he dismissed her as she offered tea or any assistance he may need. She was always taught to show respect and they would have bowed at his feet if it was necessary to make her mother healthy again.

Mr. Robson continued to explain his wife's condition to the doctor, their words began to vanish from her ears as nd they disappeared down the hallway to make way to her mother's bed-chambers. Julia sat down on the sofa twiddling her fingers as her stomach turned in knots. The anxiety about her mother's health continued to increase, but also a new feeling of which she could not describe. She hoped a new ailment was not making a way to her. Julia tilted her head back against the sofa to relieve the weakness she felt thinking she may need the doctor too. She grasped a throw pillow to her bosom and squeezed it tight for relief.

"Please help my mother," she said out loud.

"He's doing what he can, Julia," said her father walking back into the sitting room. He appeared to be a man with new confidence. "I believe we have the best doctor here in our home. He usually is punctual but was running late with his earlier home visits."

Mr. Robson left the room again after giving Julia a soothing pat on her flushed cheek. She sat up on the sofa feeling better at the touch of her father's warm hand. Desiring to make good use of her time, she walked into the kitchen next to the sitting room and poured a cup of tea from the batch they had prepared for the doctor. The warm liquid slid down her parched throat flowing down into her tumbling stomach to her delight. She no longer had the horrible thoughts of death for her mother, but a glimmer of a new spring on the horizon.

As she continued to sip the tea, she returned to the sitting room to find her father and the doctor sitting in the armchairs. They noticed her entrance and the doctor's eyes focused on Julia's face with a slight smile.

"I will be praying this works," Mr. Robson said. "If so, I will have to give you my daughter's hand in marriage."

Julia did not hear another word until she regained full composure as her entire body lay across the length of the sofa with her father and the doctor standing by her side. When she was able to lift her torso and rise to a sitting position, her father and the doctor walked back to the bedchambers of her mother.

Mr. Robson returned again. "Your mother was concerned about your condition, but I reassured her you are feeling quite well again."

∞∞∞∞

After a few weeks under the care of Dr. Clark, Mrs. Robson

began to show signs of recuperation. Julia soon learned her father was serious about his proposal for payment. She had agreed to marry this man because he cured her mother of suffering from consumption. Doctor Graham was able to conjure up a concoction of rum, boiled milk, and loaf sugar to relieve the destruction of the dreaded disease. Her poor father having no money to part with could only part with his sole daughter as payment.

As a result, the doctor became a person she loathed to see, hear or reside in his presence. She became consumed with a desire to run away from her home and escape with her diseased thoughts about him. She despised his calm demeanor and conceited confidence. She felt he took no pity on her position and to take notice of it would speak of his own weakness as a man. He knew her father would honor his word and she would do her duty as a faithful daughter for the sake of her loving mother.

They were now betrothed without any real desire for each other whether he was aware of her curious feelings or not. Julia had never desired any man and had never come close to marriage. Now, she was promised to a mere acquaintance and it was a sad reward for regaining her mother's health. She examined his expressions trying to interpret his thoughts. She did not want to make conversation with him, listen to his opinions or decipher his words. He was a future she longed to crawl away from. There was no certainty about where she was heading with him. As a young woman engaged to be married to a doctor, there was no romantic affinity for the man. Julia was intelligent, a lover of books with a bright imagination, but she could not conjure up an affection for Dr. Graham Clark. She had no definition for the type of man she desired to wed but felt an empty hole in her heart as he now defined what a husband would be for her.

Dr. Clark held a strong presence over every day of Julia's life for the next several months. It was a battle that she waged in her mind over the known love of her father and the nonexistence of love for this stranger. She wanted to beg her father to change his offer of betrothal but knew it was a self-centered appeal longing for a hint of sympathy from her father. She continued to dread each day knowing it was bringing her closer to a sealed fate taking her away from the only family she had ever known.

Dr. Clark's attitude towards Julia made her more apprehensive about the impending matrimony, heightened her girlhood fears and increased her dependency on her mother for support. She decided his conceit and vanity for respect were from his belief she swooned at the mentioning of marrying a physician from London. He had accepted that all poor young women from the countryside desired to marry a man of a higher station than their own and hoped to be his object of passion. If he had expressed some type of romance to her or spoke to her with a hint of affection, she could get accustomed to that behaviour and spoiled in the process.

However, he and her father had sealed the agreement with a handshake without a question to her opinion on the engagement. So consumed by the unnerving thought of marrying this man, Julia spent no time in planning the many outings she dreamed of partaking in with her healthy mother.

She had heard whispers in town about his flirtations with other young women and thoughts of her as a poor country lass with whom he would be disappointed as a well-known physician's wife.

When Dr. Clark came to their home to discuss the ceremony, he took no delight in her company or expressed a laugh with her maintaining a respectable distance and never attempting to stimulate her hopes of genuine affection.

"When your mother is quite well, we shall travel, Miss Robson, I shall take you to my home. The journey will relax me allowing me to be well-rested upon arrival and you shall have the opportunity to see many new places," stated Dr. Clark.

"Yes, it is time to make the preparations for the ceremony. Our neighbors and family will attend. Everyone will come and they will join us and then you can make a wonderful journey back to your estate, Dr. Clark with my beautiful daughter by your side. It shall be..."

Mr. Robson was called away by Mrs. Robson before he finished his statement and left Julia wondering what it shall be for her. She recalled what she was leaving behind. The old scenes of amusement with her dear parents, the cozy home she loved, the town she knew like no other. They were all going to be golden memories cast to the background of her mind.

Julia was leaving the sunshine of her youth for a dreary cold night away from everything she had ever known. She had no hope for a rebirth or a new beginning with this man, she lamented over the unending time she would not be able to spend with her recuperating mother. She would go to live with this stone-cold figure and live in his estate with strangers who were there to serve and please him. There was no picture of Dr. Clark's estate for her to imagine. It resided in her mind as a place for her depression to find a home. There was probably some semblance of grandeur and pomp earned as a skillful healer with the drugs and psychics he administered to his patients for her to take awe in at his request.

Awakened from her daydream by the bang of the door closing, Julia became conscious of her father walking the doctor to his waiting carriage. She dragged herself to her bedchambers and threw herself on the bed. Her head began to throb as she willed herself to sleep in hopes of leaving the walking nightmare that was now her life.

Chapter Two

Dr. Graham and Julia Clark rode down the London busy streets while their carriage driver hummed a Christmas carol. Graham pulled his curtain back allowing the city breeze to flow past Julia's worried face. They were about to engage in a new life together. Her father thought it would be the best life for her after he felt compelled to marry her off to the doctor for saving his wife's life.

"I believe it is a tad too soon for songs of Christmas cheer, Davey," yelled Dr. Clark to his driver.

In between whistled tunes from their driver, Graham would turn to Julia and ask, "Are you surviving the journey?"

Who was he to assume she had never traveled before? Every time he asked her she gave him the same reply. "I am enjoying the journey, Doctor Clark." Then she would glance out of the carriage window,

"My first name is Graham and your name is *Julia*?" asked Graham.

"Yes, I believe you know my first name," she replied.

"Then speak to me like you know mine." He cleared his throat.

Julia stared out of the window, wishing she could leave the carriage ride with this stranger. She longed to be with her recovering mother and help her regain her strength. Instead, she was being sent away to be the bride of her mother's savior.

"I have never been made to feel ashamed of my formality before," said Julia. "If you can please allow me the required time to become comfortable in your presence."

"I have no time requirement. Most women dream of falling into bed with me, as I expect you to do like my new wife tonight." Graham flashed a sly grin.

Julia noticed he was handsome before when he came by her family's home to nurse her sickly mother. Seeing his grin now, increased her fear of falling deeply for this mysterious stranger before she could get to know him well. He had no code of propriety to show her but she expected as a physician he would uphold the unspoken rules they lived by.

"I do require time if you will respect my wishes, it is deeply appreciated," said Julia. She stared straight ahead. "My father has respected you so much as to bestow you with my hand in marriage, the least you can do is respect his daughter."

"That is often the case in an arrangement such as ours. Therefore, I will give you the time you desire," said Graham as he patted her gloved hand. "However, say nothing when I do not come home at night."

Julia felt nothing when he touched her.

They traveled through London and soon made their way to their final destination. The carriage began to roll over a graveled driveway. Julia moved her curtain back to reveal thick tall trees lining the edge of the driveway. They held thick branches overhead blocking out the rays of the bright sun.

"These trees are lush and pretty," said Julia staring up at the trees

"They are not meant to be pretty. They are here to do their job. To block the harsh light of the sun."

Julia scrunched up her eyebrows as she continued to look out at the mature trees.

"I am certain I will become accustomed to them as I take in my daily strolls," replied Julia.

"I am sure you will find an abundance of obscene nature to observe here," said Graham stroking his chin. "You can walk wherever you like. However, remember you are not yet familiar with the city."

Julia sighed. "I am prepared to learn my way around with *time*."

The driver pulled the carriage up to a massive mansion. It was located on two acres of London's outskirts. The land was filled with various greenery and appeared to be unkempt. Beyond, the immediate grounds, the land gave way to the darkness of the streets they had left behind. Julia was unsure if she was brave enough to explore the city on her own.

"Is this property all yours?" asked Julia as she motioned her hand over to the estate.

"Of course it is all mine. You are free to venture around, however, I may never see you again," Graham laughed.

Julia cocked her head. "I beg your pardon, I do not find humor in your jovial display, Sir."

"If you are looking for an apology you will never find one here," Graham said turning away from her.

Julia gawked at the mansion towering before her outside of the carriage. It glared back at her with its crumbling white paint peeling down in strips. The large windows strained to shine against the overpowering layer of dust.

He ought to have bartered for a window washer and a gardener. Not a new wife.

She turned away from the overgrown trailing green tangles spilling out from all sides when she heard the driver addressing her.

"This way ma'am." The driver carried her suitcases up the steps to the wide double wooden doors.

Julia followed close behind. A small cough came up from her throat as she inhaled the dust from the outside landing.

"Are you quite well?" asked Graham following her through the front door.

"I think it is the heavy dust and something else, of which I am not acquainted with," answered Julia placing her gloved hand over her mouth.

"You will become accustomed to it soon enough."

"I am not so sure I want to," she said following the driver in the house.

A short older woman met them in the parlor. "I was not expecting guests, Dr. Graham. You should have informed me prior to allowing the proper preparations to be made."

"Yes, I should have sent word to you Edwina, but time did not permit me," said Graham in a low tone. He looked at the older woman and gave her a false smile.

Edwina rolled her eyes and returned the false smile.

"I am no good with introductions. Make your salutations and we shall go from there," said Graham in a rushed voice.

"I am Edwina, the caretaker of Dr. Graham's home. And who are you?" asked the woman in a cold tone.

"My name is Julia Robson," she said looking at the hard-wood floor. "Now, I am to go by the name of Mrs. Julia Clark,"

"What nonsense are you speaking of, missy?" asked Edwina her voice rising.

Julia stood in awkward silence.

"Are you telling me you have married the *doctor*?"

"Yes, I am the new addition to your household."

"Well, what a way to upset my household," muttered Edwina under her breath. "Follow me, ma'am."

The woman showed her to a small dim room. "This is where you will stay as Dr. Graham has not told me any different. Do not think for an instance you will stay in his quarters. If you need anything, let me know first before you pester him. Any questions?"

"No, ma'am. I wish to sleep at the moment."

"I am certain, you will need it as you have a long journey ahead being the new wife Dr. Graham." Edwina backed out of the room.

Julia was too tired to ponder her strange remarks. She put on her nightgown, lay on the small bed and sank into a deep slumber. Dreams always came to her with ease and tonight was no different.

She was strolling the tree-covered gravel path under the darkness of the tree canopy. Her back tensed with fear, but she kept walking. The density of the darkness became overpowering and she could no longer see the gravel beneath her feet.

She strained to make out a faint glimmer of light ahead. She ran to it, but it slipped from her grasp as the tree branches began to scrape her bare arms. Blood streamed down causing her to scream out in pain then she woke up from the sound leaving her throat.

Julia's heart attempted to beat out of her chest as she lay there in shock. Sleep would not return. She never had night sweats, but the temperature in the room rose to an unbearable heat level. She had to go outside where the crisp air would cool her feverish face.

Was I running from this mansion or to it?

"I am a new bride in a large neglected mansion and unsure of this new life," she said out loud as she walked on the outside landing.

Feeling her anxiety subside, Julia turned around to return to her new bedchambers. Out of the corner of her eye, she noticed a shadow move around the corner of the landing. She stopped in her steps. She listened for footsteps but heard none. She took a step, stopped and listened again, to hear only the rustling of leaves blowing in the trees. Feeling fear take over, she raced to her new room, locked the door and hid under the covers.

Chapter Three

J ulia could not sleep and prayed for daybreak to arrive. She dressed for the day hoping the routine would calm her. She went to the large dining hall where the walls were filled with old paintings. She gazed at the paintings as she waited to be served sitting at a long table, and surprised to be eating alone. Edwina walked in from the kitchen along with a younger woman wearing an apron.

"Good morning, ma'am," she said in a cheerful voice. "I am Ada Dillon, the cook. I have prepared your breakfast."

She placed a plate of eggs, toast, and bacon before Julia. It smelled delicious.

"Thank you so much, Ada."

"It is a pleasure, ma'am."

"Please call me Julia." She picked up her fork taking a bite full of eggs. She did not realize how famished she was on her journey.

"If you insist, ma'am," said Ada standing beside a dining chair. "How was your first night in the Clark mansion?"

"Not the best. I believe I am exhausted from everything that has happened. I had the strangest dream," replied Julia as she buttered her toast.

Edwina gave a slight grin.

Julia did not return the grin. She felt uneasy under Edwina's focus. She continued to eat in silence.

"Is Dr. Clark joining me for breakfast?" Asked Julia breaking the uncomfortable moments of silence.

"He has already eaten breakfast with us in the kitchen. We are early risers and do not eat with guests," said Edwina sticking her chin out.

"I am not a guest. I am a member of the household now. Will I always have to eat in solitude?" Julia gave a small laugh.

Edwina failed to answer.

Julia glanced at a painting on the wall at the end of the dining room. It contained a well-dressed family. A curly-haired baby boy sat on the lap of a pretty young woman. She had a glum look on her face as the baby smiled up at her.

"Who are they?" asked Julia pointing to the painting.

"Ask your new husband. This is his home where he holds all of the secrets," Edwina said as she left the dining room.

Julia tried hard to swallow the bit of bacon she just put in her mouth. She struggled not to look at the painting as she ate to avoid the man's cold eyes that made her shiver.

Despite the certainty of knowing she was now the doctor's wife, her timidness and insecurity continued to plague her. The words she struggled to think of to make conversation never made it to her tongue. She was conflicted in her choice to make an agreement to love her new home or hold it in contempt and deny it's permanence. She trembled under the study of Edwina but hungered for some type of friendship from these women. She listened to them make a few quiet remarks about the duties of their day, but she listened as a foreign witness, not a trusted family member.

Julia had not been in the presence of Dr. Clark and she did

enjoy his absence for the morning. She did not miss his mean playfulness making her feel small, so she decided to spend the day wandering and strolling around the grounds. She would enjoy the bright daylight before she would end up back in the lonesome darkroom of her bedchambers. She had been sure to bring her books for some form of amusement but she found no pleasure in reading them. As she sat at the head of the long dining room table, she longed to weep not for her suffering but because she was alone. The dread of her daily life in this drab estate was too much to bear for her heart. She sensed a deep anguished pain to the depths of her being and was resigned to the fact she would walk around in a cloud of depression for the rest of the days of her life. There was nothing she could do to change her plot and had the faint glimmer of her father's happy hopes for her.

She recalled his words as she packed to leave his home, "My daughter will make a beautiful doctor's wife. I did not waste my years in grooming you to be the wife of a peasant. You are a blessing to me and I shall not despair in making this decision for you."

A lone tear fell from her eye.

"You will find the garden quite lovely, ma'am," said Ada in a soft tone. "You may decide to take up the art of growing some pretty things in there. It's a pity I don't have the gift for it."

"Your gift is in this kitchen, Mary," said Edwina in a bitter voice as she strolled away from the table.

"You would want me to be selfish with my gifts, Edwina. I can do other things too. I don't have a narrow mind. The world can use a good heart and good hands. Remember, ma'am, that's where your happiness lies."

"I must remember your wise words, Mary," replied Julia.

Was she being as selfish as Dr. Clark with her feelings? She clung to the selfishness of her pain and sadness, something stronger than his. He was free from any fears or doubts for his future, she was deep in it, a longing for torture to end. Was this a bond they shared? Selfishness?

Should she provide him pity, love; a subtle influence to make him feel her mental caress?

∞∞∞

Julia left the dining room feeling full and looked at more of the artwork. She wondered where her new husband was and why he would not give her a personal tour. She walked the hallways noticing the peeling paint and stained cracks.

"This mansion is not doing well," Julia muttered.

"Maybe, you are here to make it better."

Julia jumped as she heard the voice of Graham standing in the doorway of one of the many rooms.

"I was talking to myself, Sir. I must admit it is one of my silly habits."

"I must continue to listen in doorways to hear your hidden secrets then," said Graham as he motioned for her to enter the room.

"I hope you do not mind me saying, but your home needs attention," said Julia as she sat down in a weathered brown leather chair.

"I think it has character," said Graham sitting across from her at a desk.

"The character it displays may not be the most pleasant."

Graham smiled.

"Do you find me unpleasant?"

Thrown by his question, Julia looked away and felt her cheeks growing warm.

"You can tell me. After all, I am your husband now," he said looking directly at her.

"You are cordial...enough," stammered Julia. "You are a physician and you must have some care for the welfare of others."

"Precisely. I come from a family of apothecaries and surgeons that have cared for others," he said looking at papers on his desk. "But I have risen to the level of a respected physician."

Julia perked up. "Like the family in the painting in the dining room?"

"I am the small babysitting on the lap of my mother with my father at her side. He grew up in Derbyshire, became a London surgeon and planted our family here in this mansion left to him by a member of the Ton because he saved the life of one them after sawing off their leg."

"Oh my," Julia gasped and decided to change the subject from the gruesomeness of an amputation. "You were a precious baby, Sir."

"I can still be precious," he said eyeing her reaction.

She blushed and looked at his desk.

"My blushing bride. How sweet is this moment?"

Julia could not speak.

"I was a precious baby, but what was not sweet, is the family in the painting. It happened to capture one moment and that is all. Do you have any further questions?"

"Yes, Sir."

"Please refrain from calling me, Sir. I am your husband. Call me Graham."

"All right, *Graham*."

"I can begin to enjoy the sound of your lovely voice saying my name many times," he laughed. "Your question, Julia?"

"I do not mean to offend you, but you are a doctor. It is not becoming of a man of your status to live in this manner. Why do you keep your home in such ill repair?" asked Julia continuing to look at his desk and noticing the chipped wood.

"This mansion is quite old. There is a story behind it, but now is not the time to indulge you."

Julia looked at him. "I thought we were discussing secrets as you say."

Graham squirmed in his chair.

"It is important you understand I am a professional and I allow my head to lead me, but I do have a heart too," he aimed his finger at his chest. "Although I endeavor to forget about it on a daily basis."

He gave her a speech on the medical profession. She paid attention to his words when she would rather have turned him away. She chose not to do it. He walked around the desk and took her pointer finger and aimed it at her head and then to her own heart. She could not resist how warm his finger felt against her hand. He glided into her personal space, leaving a hint of a romantic overtone.

"I have ideas." He pulled papers from his desk. "See, ma'am, I am thinking of a future."

"Thank you for sharing it with me," said Julia. "I hope you do not feel obligated to entertain me."

Was that the correct response? She smoothed her hand

across the paper. She tingled at the crispness imagining how Graham poured his energy over them. She faced Graham, tingles moving from her fingers to other parts of her body.

"There are other places I could be right now, but I am rather enjoying the view I have in my own house." He chuckled. "We will be creators together after all."

Julia grimaced, "I think it is best I give you your privacy to work."

"No, give me your attention, we can create many things together. Come with me."

They spent an hour going from floor to floor as Julia felt no more creative than when they started. She looked at Graham with a weary smile.

He let out a laugh, "Take it all in. You need a moment?"

Julia turned to step away from Graham. It wasn't just the mansion. It was having to live with such an intoxicating stranger such as Dr. Graham Clark.

She could not allow this man's spell to overwhelm her. One moment he was being obnoxious and the next he was showing depth. She turned to look at his wavy, thick hair as he was focusing on the blueprints he held up against the wall. She breathed in and stepped next to him.

He looked at her and smiled. He lowered the papers down from the wall.

"Do not look at me in that manner. It is frustrating."

With a raised eyebrow he asked, "Frustrating? Why?"

She could tell he was enjoying every second. His simple smile had control over her but Julia denied revealing this thought to him. "I hardly know you. We need time to become acquainted in the proper manner. You do have the upper hand, but I also have some say in the matter."

Graham's smile disappeared. "Calm yourself, Julia. I know this is all new to you. It will work out in the end. You did not ask for this and neither did I."

"I am as calm as I can be under the circumstances, Sir." Julia could pretend she knew how to relax with Graham around. She knew a lot was riding on this marriage, not to mention her future here in the mansion. Julia pulled her thick curls back from her tensing forehead and let them spring forward. "I really have to get back to my chambers and I am sure you have patients to see."

Graham stopped walking for a moment. "All right, I will take leave of you. You are correct, I have patients to attend to in the city and my driver, Davis, will take me momentarily. You may enjoy the premises in my absence," said Graham as he went back to his office to grab his black doctor bag and leave for a London hospital.

Before he left, he looked at her hard, walked away to the front door to leave the mansion and turned on his heels. He was headed back in her direction. He looked down at his black bag and then leaned in to place his hand on her trembling hand. His aftershave drifting over to her. Why did he have to smell so good? She soon recalled the same scent from the previous carriage ride. The warm touch of his large hand heated up her uneasy grasp. She also remembered how his whole body had been a cozy warmth to sit next to on the saddle seat. The memories flooded her thoughts.

Graham lingered a moment without speaking.

Then speaking slowly. "If you insist I take leave of you, I can do that." Graham headed for the doors leading to the carriage.

She looked down at her hand wondering what to do with it. Just the feel of his hand in hers and knowing Graham had held it was enough to make her melt. She stared at the doorway he had just walked through. The room looked lonely without him standing there. Thoughts like this would not get the best of her. This grim mansion was enough to deal with.

Julia took firm hold of her hand, paying little attention to the soft feel of her, but attempting to recapture the firmness of his. She was going to handle this new marriage in a proper fashion. There was no other choice. Her family depended on it.

Julia shook her head from side to side and sat in a chair in the hallway staring at the foyer. She sat for fifteen minutes taking in the fading paint, books piled on the floor of the hallway, pieces of paper thrown in the corners and weird sharp objects were strewn in a pile at the entry of the sitting room.

What kind of life am I going to have here?

Chapter Four

The next morning, Ada served breakfast alone without Edwina. Julia was pleased and felt more comfortable talking to a young lady closer to her age.

"She was a beautiful woman, but she does appear to be sad. Do you know who she was?" asked Julia pointing at the painting with her fork.

Ada sat down at the table with her. "Keep your voice low, you never know who may be listening."

"If you are referring to Dr. Clark. I saw him leave for the day. However, I know he listens in doorways," said Julia raising her eyebrows.

"There are ears everywhere. Be mindful of what you say and to whom you say it to."

"I know Edwina is not happy about my arrival. I will stand my guard with her. Can you tell me about the painting?"

"Well, her name was Victoria and your husband's mother. His father was having an affair with the child's nurse. She was always well-poised, but resigned to her place in life as his wife in name only."

"Now, I understand the sadness."

"Her sadness increased when the nurse became pregnant with her husband's child. They did manage to keep it well hidden from everyone in town. The doctor's father was so smitten with the young nurse, he resorted to poisoning his wife to live alone with his lover," said Ada in a low voice.

"What a horrid thing to do," said Julia. She stared at the woman's sad eyes in the painting. "And who raised little Graham?"

"My Aunt Edwina came here to help raise him," said Ada placing her elbows on the table.

"I did not know she was your aunt," replied Julia. "I apologize if I offended you with my thoughtless opinion of her."

"I take no offense. I know she is as hard as the cement walls of this mansion. She was also the sister of the nurse, Ella," she rested her face in her hand.

"She chose to live here and take care of her sister's lover's child, it is unbelievable," Julia said resting her fork on the plate. "What happened to the nurse's baby and the nurse?"

"My mother died in childbirth and you're looking at little baby Mary," she said in a flat tone.

Julia gasped.

"The bodies of both women are buried here on the grounds," said Ada rubbing her temples.

Julia opened her eyes wide and her mouth dropped open.

"No need to fear the dead. I have heard they both had beautiful spirits"

"Why?" asked Julia.

"They seek to haunt the source of their pain," responded Mary. "This is the story handed down to me."

Julia gave Ada a weak smile.

"Have I answered your question about the portrait, Mrs.

Julia?" asked Ada pointing at the portrait.

"You can call me Julia because you *are* my sister-in-law as you've disclosed to me."

"In a sense, however, I do not push the fact because I am an unwanted child from an unmarried woman. Dr. Graham and I are half-siblings. He allows me and my Aunt Edwina to live here and to help take care of them."

"*Them?* Who is them? Who else is living here?"

"I know Dr. Graham would *love* to tell you about his house. I do not know much about your background, but I was told he saved your sick mother from the brink of death. Although you come from different worlds, you may have much in common."

"I do not understand."

"I have overstepped my bounds. It is not my place, I am here to cook for you," said Ada pushing back her chair.

"No, you have not, Mary. I would like for us to be friends. I could use one in this dismal place," said Julia looking up at Ada as she stood up.

"I do not want to give you false hope, but you deserve to have good things to come from your situation. That is precisely why you are here."

"You have enlightened me, to say the least. However, I now feel enveloped in sadness."

"There is a great deal of grief. Maybe, you can change it by bringing new life into this home."

"So, I am a fortunate wife?"

"I try to think I am most fortunate. It is my story too after all. Let me know when you meet our Christmas spirits."

"I do not believe in spirits. However, I'm uncomfortable

with bodies buried on the land I live on," said Julia. She gave a nervous laugh.

"That is quite funny, Mrs. Julia," said Ada looking hard at Julia. "I do not believe you will be able to move them. If you don't mind, I have work to do."

"Thank you for telling me about your sad, gruesome tale. I think I will partake in a walk in the sunshine now."

Julia had to get some air.

Why did I ask about the portrait again?

Chapter Five

Dr. Graham Clark was respected in London. He did not maintain the family estate, also known as Clark Mansion, but the city needed a physician to work in their hospital and he was one of the few they had.

Dr. George Clark had moved his small family into the vast property when he took Lady Victoria as his wife. She soon bore him a son, whom he took no great affinity to.

He soon became Sir George Clark and lived a life of access to luxury. His reputation was stellar in town and he was intent on maintaining it. His wandering eye often betrayed him. His wife was often cold and it was not for lack of love, it was due to her fear of his verbal crudeness.

He paid adequate attention to their budding little toddler and Victoria was grateful for his devotion. She had a distaste for his nighttime affairs and was not quite content with being alone. She had a place in society and she knew many ladies in town suffered as she did, but she was different. She wanted real love and desired no pity for her plight. She had found someone to love, her beautiful baby boy, Graham.

The household staff loved Victoria and her baby boy, but they feared Sir George Clark. He was a stern dictator and nothing could please him. Lady Victoria, unlike her George, was even-tempered and developed close relationships with the servants.

They remained at Clark Mansion because of the kindness of Victoria. Most of all they could not resist the sweet laughter of little Master Graham. He was beginning to walk when his nurse, Sarah moved away with her new husband. However, she informed Lady Victoria of a fine replacement.

However, when Victoria laid eyes on beautiful Miss Ella, she wrapped her days and nights in worry. She did not want the young lady to fall victim to her George, but she liked Sarah and gave in to the request for employment for Miss Ella.

∞∞∞∞

Graham Clark always pondered the story he had heard from Edwina as he grew older. He contrasted it with the crass remarks his father always told him. As a result, he was torn. Find true love and be happy, or be happy and love whoever you find for the moment.

Dr. Graham Clark made his rounds to patients during the day and to his mistresses during the night. They were never serious affairs, just available entertainment to pass the time.

He had plenty of young misses at his disposal. His new wife, Julia, was unaware of his pursuits. She was from a township far from London. However, word had spread of his new beautiful bride as he was informed by the family member of a young patient.

He began to notice Mrs. Julia Clark as a lovely and well-polished 21-year-old despite her previous station in life. Silently admiring her flattering well-trimmed figure, he could not help his increased curiosity the more he saw her walking the premises.

What was Graham thinking? How would this pretty young lady live in his dilapidated mansion? Graham knew the type of husband Julia deserved. He could not fit the mold. Maybe he would not pay her any affectionate attention since he was hardly home. He could lose himself in the dark estate during the small amount of time he was there. This was the most he could hope for.

"How is your lovely new bride enjoying life in London?" asked Mr. Woodland.

"I will be certain to make a full inquiry upon my return home for you."

"Yes, do let me know," he said with a chuckle.

Dr. Graham Clark revealed a slight grin.

$$\infty\infty\infty$$

"Julia?"

"Sir?"

"Ah, *Julia*, I'm beginning to become enthralled with how your name rolls off my tongue. I want to say it more and more."

"Thank you...sir," said Julia as her cheeks blushed bright pink.

"*Sir*? I have informed you about that. We must become well acquainted. I am Dr. Graham Clark, but also your husband and new lover," he said with a slow lick of his lips.

"I am your bride, but it would be quite improper for me to hear such words." Julia stood up from her bed. "We hardly know each other."

"Mrs. Clark, I must insist on being improper," he said letting out a laugh.

Julia looked into his dark eyes. Graham's overwhelming presence was filling her small bedchambers.

"I am certain you will enjoy our time together, Julia," he said walking closer to her.

"I require sleep, sir. I insist you take leave of me," Julia said standing.

"When we are done getting acquainted," he said stepping closer to her.

Passion was building between them. The first gaze into his steel dark eyes was making her feel warmer by the moment. She did not know if she could get out of his presence without falling for him.

Julia could not resist the hardness of his arms. She was excited by how her soft slender arms looked against the thickness of his. There was a clear approval from her. He knew to trust it. He had moments like this before and knew how they would succumb to his touch.

She had to stabilize her thoughts before she fell for him. "Why are we doing this?"

"We are doing this because we can."

"Well, when you are alone, will you want me in your bedchamber?"

He stared at her, his mind skimming the many nights that he had spent with other ladies. "I have enjoyed my time alone and reminiscing memories."

"I do not know you well enough to believe you."

"I do not ask for your belief."

"There is nothing lonelier than a man who can have it all but chooses otherwise. You are utterly sad, Graham," she said as he held her close.

They could make a connection. It could be real. She wanted to ease her poverty filled life away. She wanted to ease his grief-filled life away. Julia decided to make the best choice for her future pulling his face down to hers, allowing their lips to find each other with light kisses to the touch.

They did not remain easy for long feeling comfortable, building heat between them. Their mouths growing wide and their tongues dancing to the silence.

She hung to him for balance. He held her and they melted into the curves of their bodies. The coldness of the mansion was forgotten as he warmed to her soft body.

He gently released her body from his and motioned to her small bed. "Now is the time, Julia."

He led the way. She prayed in her heart for them to develop a true connection. He was looking for love and she could give it. They fell into a solid embrace, kissing long and hard.

"This feels so wonderful," Julia mumbled.

She gripped his head, letting her fingers play with his thick black hair as their bodies danced together.

"I can't take this. I need you," he said as he backed her into the bed.

She gave him a tantalizing smile much to her surprise.

Chapter Six

Feeling happy about her night with Graham, Julia decided to take a walk after he left for his day. She walked out of her room and heard a door slam with a loud bang many doors down the long dark hall.

Julia heard a man laugh. A boisterous, deep laugh echoed far down the hall from her. She jumped not expecting to hear a man's voice after Graham left. She thought maybe he had returned after forgetting one of his drugs for his many patients. She decided to walk toward the laughing, hoping to get a warm kiss from her doctor husband.

The darkness of the hallway caused her to reach for a candle and light it in the dimly lit hallway, but the laughing stopped. The light of a small window further away allowed a sliver of sunlight to enter. Julia focused on the welcome light.

"Graham, have you returned?" Julia asked her voice sounding small in the long hallway.

A high pitched wail came from behind Julia. Then she heard banging on the wall. She turned, running for her chambers. As she passed the staircase, she glimpsed Edwina on the staircase bending over and holding her foot.

"Edwina?" Julia asked going down to her.

"Yes, it is me. I banged my foot on the step," Edwina replied rubbing her toes. "I should be used to the dimness by now."

"Are you going to see Graham?" asked Julia.

"Why would you ask me that?" She looked at Julia with wide eyes. "He left to go and treat his patients."

"Impossible. I heard him laughing down the hall," said Lindsey.

"Your Dr. Clark?"

"Yes, who else would I be referring to?" asked Julia. She let out a nervous laugh.

"Well, have you forgotten about Sir Clark? Ada did not provide the full history?"

Julia's hand began to tremble as she held onto the railing. Nobody told her about him. Was he living here too?

"You ain't scared of our Sir Clark are you?"

"If I was scared, would I be walking the halls in the darkness?" asked Julia.

"Maybe, you are still sleeping alone, correct?" asked Edwina. She spoke with a tone of accusation.

Julia shrugged her shoulders. "I will allow you to pursue your chores."

Edwina gave a deep sigh. "Be mindful of the dark, missy. You may step where you are not wanted."

Julia did not reply and walked back to her room.

"Ada has your breakfast. Eat it before it goes cold," yelled Edwina from the bottom of the staircase. "Unless you are too afraid to leave your bedchambers now, ma'am."

"I am not afraid and I will be down shortly," replied Julia in a stern voice.

"Yes, you are afraid," Edwina said to herself.

Chapter Seven

J ulia began to love being able to lounge in the mansion with Graham at her side during the night. He was spending more time with her every day. She enjoyed her tableside conversations with Ada, who always made sure she had someone to converse with and provide delicious healthy meals for her to make sure she was well fed. After all, she was now the wife of a doctor.

One cold midafternoon in early December, Julia became restless. She did not like the darkness of the mansion and longed to liven it up with holiday cheer and bring light into it. She decided to head for the kitchen to speak with Ada about it. As she approached the area, she saw a dim light coming from Edwina's room.

We need to become friends at some point.

"I would like to get your opinion. Can I borrow a moment of your time?" said Julia in a loud voice.

As Julia was about to turn into the room, it went dark.

"Are you sleeping now?" asked Julia in a soft voice.

She received no reply but looked in the darkroom, trying to adjust her eyes to the darkness. The room appeared to be empty.

"Edwina?" Julia whispered. "Did your candle go out?"

She left the room and walked out of the front door. As she neared the landing to go around to where she saw the figure before. She stopped and peered around the corner. She tried to focus her eyes in the darkness as the mansion cast a dark shade on the garden.

Julia listened for footsteps, but only heard the sound of her breathing.

Sir Clark?

She kept close to the mansion as she tiptoed around to the back peering the chilly darkness in hopes of finding Edwina, but nobody was there.

∞∞∞

Ada was nudging Julia to wake up with one hand and holding a glass of orange juice in the other.

"I have been sleeping so well now," said Julia opening her eyes and smiling as she thought about her passion-filled nights with Graham.

"I'm so pleased for you, Mrs. Julia," said Ada as she placed the glass in Julia's hand. "You skipped breakfast and I did not want you to sleep through lunch too."

She sipped the orange juice. "I keep hearing or seeing things during the day around here though."

"What things?" asked Ada raising her eyebrows.

"Sounds like someone is walking around the corner in front of me or there are candlelights where there should be none."

Julia gave Ada a quizzical look. "Edwina told me Sir Clark lives here. Your father, maybe it is him. I have yet to make his acquaintance."

"I cannot speak about it. You have not asked your husband about him?"

"I cannot find the right moment to bring it up with him," said Julia as she sat up in the bed. "I have found peace in this marriage and I am happy with what I have with Graham. I do not want to create new problems with us."

"It tis good to see you accepting your role as the doctor's wife and all. I am sure it was quite difficult leaving your family behind. We all have to bear a heavy load for our family at times. I have my own. As you know I never cook for the old man," whispered Mary. "I have heard bad things about him, but I want to believe they are all rubbish. When I am here, I have had *no* issues and I certainly do not see my father. I have no relationship with him."

"I do not understand why you do not know your father. I adore my father and miss him dearly. Graham and Edwina have not talked to you about him?" asked Julia.

"No, they have not. You are blessed to have a loving father and mother. I have not been so fortunate. This mansion swallows love wholly and spit out darkness. Why do you think the doctor keeps it like this?"

Julia shook her head from side to side. "I cannot bring myself to ask him but the subject saddens me for his sake."

"He is grieving his mother and so am I, but we each handle it in our own manner."

"You both are grieving your father too, I believe. Is he here?"

"If he is here, he must not want anything to do with me," said Ada wiping a lone tear from her cheek.

"There is too much sadness. I have a wonderful idea, we will go to find him, that is simple enough, it will be for Christmas," said Julia rising from the bed. "We will do this for you and

Graham."

"Mrs. Julia I do not want you to trouble yourself with our old family unpleasantness," she pats Julia on the shoulder.

"No, I want you to meet him. We have to lift the dark cloud from this estate," she said.

Ada looked at Julia with a look of concern. "I have to go with you. Who knows what Edwina will do to you if you are out there alone sneaking around. Where shall we start?"

"Alright, but I do not want to barge in his room when we find it. Let's make it look as we are bringing him some orange juice," she said holding up her half-filled glass.

"I will follow your lead, Mrs. Julia," replied Ada. "Let us hurry before my aunt gets suspicious about my absence."

As Julia and Ada crossed the staircase to make their way down the hall, they met Edwina.

"Where are you two heading?" she asked with a look of disdain.

"I am taking Ada to see her father," said Julia smiling.

"Her father?" Edwina asked in a high pitched voice.

"Yes, and you are wrong. I am not afraid."

"I would be afraid of your husband's anger for being as nosey as you are."

"Why?" asked Julia feeling hot tears come to her eyes.

"You will run your off husband back to the arms of other women with your probing," Edwina spat turning up her nose at Julia.

"Aaah, Mrs. Julia, I will leave the issue alone," said Ada patting Julia on the back. "My duties await me as I belong in the kitchen, now."

Julia watched Ada run down the staircase as she fought back tears.

"Keep your nose out of your husband's personal affairs," hissed Edwina. "You should be thankful for having a physician to live with instead of looking in dark places where you do not belong."

"Lunch will be ready soon, Mrs. Julia," yelled Ada from the bottom of the staircase. "I know you must be famished."

"Not at this time," she answered with a look of defeat. "How long must I live in this dark ugly place?"

"I thought you would have longed to live in a mansion with a handsome husband. It is what every young girl dreams of I believe."

"Possibly a long time ago dreaming in my family's cottage," Julia said with a look of disappointment. "However, this is not quite what I expected."

"Nothing ever is," Edwina hissed over her shoulder as she descended the stairs.

Chapter Eight

As the temperature became colder outside, so did the atmosphere within the Clark estate. Dr. Graham Clark consumed the waking thoughts of Julia as he sometimes was an enigma or at other times absorbed her every emotion. She was surrounded by a trust and a distrust for him, a love and a lust for him. He continued to be playful in tone and held superiority over her intoxicating her mind as well as frustrating it. Julia did not feel at ease during the day, but completely comfortable by his warm side at night. His inner self remained covered by a shroud and he only expressed himself in a language of physical love and composure. She wondered if she pleased him and longed to hear his affections and see his smiles. However, she desired to get past the questions of the secrets about his father. There was a strong avoidance of the topic that pained her heart and she could feel crushing his soul.

However, Julia was eager to spend any blissful days with him without the cloud of his family secret hovering over her head. She wanted no estrangement between them and no mystery or doubts to absorb their new love allowing it to be free to flourish. She accepted him as the perfect partner, a good provider and an upstanding member of society. This could turn out so good for her.

She forced her throat to swallow as she practiced how she would request to meet her father-in-law. Returning an easy smile to her gaze in the mirror, pretending to look at Graham, she held out her hand to her reflection hoping for him to reciprocate in her fantasy. She did not care if he refused to introduce her to his father, he would have no choice but to do right by her and give in to her request.

Julia looked at her open hand, racing emotions swept across her face. Indecision was one of them. Feeling a pang of guilt about putting him on the spot, she glanced at her reflection revealing a young schoolgirl with an air of vulnerability and anguish. Julia blinked back the hot tears determined to fall down her cheeks.

Later that night, Julia lay in her bed waiting nestled under the warm blankets. She loved their time alone in her room. It was their sanctuary and a place where she could be adored by her new husband. He had been visiting her almost every night for the past couple of months, but he had not yet taken her to his bedchambers.

Tonight, I will ask him.

Julia could feel her cheeks growing warm as she heard the sound of his boots on the hardwood floor outside her door. He was coming to their lovemaking haven.

"My lovely *Julia*?"

Her skin tingled as he whispered her name easing open the door.

"Yes, my love," she said with a slight smile. "I do have a question for you."

He rushed to her side.

"Your question can wait, I must have your delicate body now, my lovely *Julia*."

Chapter Nine

G raham left the warm home of his recuperating patient and went out into the frigid evening air. The blast of air exacerbated an already excruciating headache from the night before as a result of Julia's heartfelt plea. He kept trying to figure out a way without having to explain his father's predicament to his new bride.

The city of London was deep in an icy freeze, while the sky blazed a purple-blue haze. Graham could not help but marvel at the arrangement of colors in the vastness above him. He stood for a few moments, gazing up, secretly hoping to fly away. He imagined being suspended on the cool breeze flying through the gray clouds. He brought his gaze down to the busy city streets. He stared down the grimy road as far as his eyes could travel looking for a suggestion to take a different route to the unknown where he would not have to face what was waiting for him at home.

The stiff English wind was circulating down among the Christmas holly entwined on the many light poles as the flicker from the newly lit candles strained to light the way of the busy Londoners. Graham could feel the chill on his neck down to his fingertips. He pulled his coat collar closer. The only light in the dark carriage came from the lantern of the driver, but Graham knew the way well.

The city life of London drifted farther away as Graham made his way home as a devoted husband should. He moved the curtain back to take in a few last glimpses of the city he adored until familiar tall trees came into view and became his point of interest. That was his home. Graham was always accustomed to the feeling of anxious anticipation upon reaching his estate, but now a new air of curiosity coursed through his veins about what was there to meet him.

∞∞∞

"Taking your time to show up huh, Graham? You think you are going to be rid of me soon because of your pretty young bride," said the old man.

Edwina was grinning at Graham while the old man gave him a fierce stare as he made his way to the large bed. He had to feign confidence as if nothing had changed or they would discover his private torment.

"My days are long at times," Graham said. "Do you not remember?"

"So you say," the old man let out a loud laugh. "I thought you gave up your weak patients to spend time with your new bride like the good husband you pretend to be."

Graham gave a hard stare to the man. He recalled for a split second who he used to be. His father represented his earlier apathetic self. His stomach turned over on itself and made him want to vomit. It was beyond the hour he wanted to be with them. Time was whispering its existence away as the full moon hung in the night air. He could not forget Julia was waiting for him. He looked in the direction of the door and envisioned her smile as he walked into her room always appearing angelic.

His body moved towards the door, but he stepped back fearful his motive would be apparent to them. He had to take his time and endure his father's tirade of insanity.

∞∞∞

Forcing his throat to swallow, Graham managed to release an easy smile for Julia and held his hand out to her, forcing her to reciprocate. He did not care if she wanted to or not, but he would leave the choice in her hands. Julia looked at his open hand, emotions filled with anxiety, swept across her face.

Graham felt a pang of guilt for leaving her without an answer to her question last night. He thought she might like the open gesture after their night of pleasure. He decided to leave early while she was sleeping to rid the excuses he would have to come up with believing she would never understand his predicament.

"I need light and air in this place. You may need to find someone else from town to live here as your wife. I cannot live in this place any longer." She stood up to leave the room. "I cannot live with the dark secrets this place holds."

Graham considered going after her but stayed, then moved to step in front of her with several swift motions of his long legs. He stood like a statue.

She froze her brown eyes on his steel-blue eyes, without a hint of invitation. "I will take leave of you, Doctor, allow me to pass."

He had hurt her and she would not accept it.

"Allow me more time to explain, Julia."

She looked up at him. "You did not ask for time this morning. I thought you had no answers for me."

He rubbed his temples with his fingers. "We had a lovely

night and we need not ruin it with this intense departure."

Julia looked to the side.

He was guilt-stricken and lowered his face toward the floor.
Her lips quivered. "You say things like that to all of your female liaisons?"

Yes, he knew how to apply the charm. However, Julia's beautiful personality made his bow to hers.

He should not make her suffer for it.

Graham softened his voice, "You may not believe this, but my father is insane. He killed my mother to be with his lover and ended up losing her as well. He wants me and everyone else to suffer. Including Clark Mansion and his daughter. He relishes the darkness because he cannot bring himself to face her or his inner demons. He is an angry, bitter shell of a man."

Julia strained to glance at him through her tears now blinding her sight.

Graham let out a sigh because he failed to treat his father's sickness. He drew in a deep gulp of air before speaking again. "I apologize for holding back my secrets from you. I have taken you to a dark place you were not prepared to go."

"I will go there with you and I will accept your humility. I cannot leave you because you need me and I need you but there is work for us to be done before we can proceed in this family."

"I do not think we can work through this."

"You are mistaken. You must have faith in love and learn to believe in us as I have done. You know, I have been thinking of a project for you and a better way of life for your father and your patients. "

"I do not understand, maybe you have been living in this darkness too long, my dear. Why would I start a project to anger my father or abandon the urgent needs of my patients and their families? You remember how much you and your father needed my help with your mother's illness. I can support them without you, my dear. I am good at providing adequate care to those in need before you came into my life. Edwina and Ada can attest to that fact."

Julia's brown eyes moistened. "You would rather please others at the destruction of your very soul?"

"If you were to peer into my dark inkling of a soul, you may see a disgraceful picture."

"I have seen many glimpses of the caring soul you have shown me. However, I want it to shine and I want to shine with it, but it cannot beam one ray of light in this sanctuary of gloom. I desire for our love to grow or I can live here no longer, Graham."

He saw the determination in her stance, she would not back down. Julia stood in stony silence wringing her hands back and forth.

"What do you have in mind for this project?"

"We can create a bright, clean sanctuary in a wing of your mansion for your patients to get healthy and a place for your father to find peace," beamed Julia. "We can right after Christmas Day."

"Your idea sounds delightful for my patients because I have seen the sloth and filth they are forced to deal with in those hospital beds. Believe me, there is no Christmas cheer in that place. My father, on the other hand, is a beast that cannot be tamed by bright lights and cleanliness. He will not stand for it. He wants no peace, only dismay for all of us."

"You talk about the things he wants, so he keeps this crumbling mansion, but what about you?"

"Yes, I have mere dreams, like the memories of my dearly

departed mother. My father is so overwhelming, just like a renovation of this struggling estate would be for us."

"We can do it, Graham," she said with a gleam in her eye. "Let's turn it around and give your father a mission in a positive direction for the new year. He will have a purpose and still remain important as the patriarch of this family."

"You are not acquainted with my father, and do not know you will be dealing with a strong-willed monster."

"Yes, but he knows how to love, he has done it before. Where love existed before, it can grow again, but for a different purpose."

"I believe you will give up on love and on me after all of this over. We will see how this goes with my father. I am willing to change this mansion for the better. I am weary of living in his haven of despair as well."

"Can I meet him tomorrow?"

Graham relaxed his stance. "Yes, you will meet him tomorrow."

Julia walked out of the room.

"Where are you going, my love?" asked Graham standing in the doorway of her quarters.

"To bed with my husband in his bedchambers," she said twisting her hips as her determined stride revealed.

"No, it is too close to my father's quarters. I do not feel comfortable taking you there," said Graham walking after her.

Julia continued walking. "I do not know where I am going if I have to open every room to find your bedchambers, I will do it. The project begins tonight."

"I will lead the way, Julia. I must say, you are the perfect match for me, determined to do good for others in the midst of chaos. So let us begin," he took her hand and led her down the hallway to his quarters.

He recalled their many nights before in her small bed. His eyes closed, pleased with how confident his new wife had become over the last few months. They would have a large bed to play in from now on and he could not wait to take part in the project.

Chapter Ten

J ulia sat down with a thud at the long table in the dining room to drink a cup of tea. She did not sleep well, tossing and turning throughout the night, nervous about the impending meeting with Sir Clark.

"You came down to eat early today," said Graham strolling into the dining room to take a seat beside her.

Wonderful, he was going to eat breakfast with her. Graham was becoming more like a husband to her outside of her bedchambers. She grew accustomed to his changed behavior in the bed, but now he was showing a change in attitude in daylight too. The last thing she wanted was to complain to him about her restless night in his bed for the first time.

She knew his support was real and she would do all she could to support him in return for his trust. She never played with love and had devoted herself to trusting her father to send her as a token of repayment for saving her mother's life. She loved her father and knew he had her best interest in mind. Making this work marriage work would be the best gift she could give her father.

Graham knew how to love too. He missed the love of his mother but respected the tough love of his father. It was the most recent love he had known and it came with a price. One he was willing to pay today.

As Graham poured himself a cup of tea, his broad smile melted her heart as much as the piping hot tea. He was as handsome as the first time she saw him at her mother's bedside. She closed her eyes to capture him in her mind as she sipped the warm tea feeling it glide down to her chest and deepen her love glow. She hoped to feel the affection of love from Graham forever and allow it to spread throughout the estate.

She looked over at him again and noticed a bit of new irritation in his eyes. There was still the hard work of the day to be done. Julia and Graham had to overcome a barrier to end the constant wave of past grief within the home. It would always be there, looming wide in their future life, if they did not battle and destroy it together.

"Do not worry, we will keep the faith when talk with your father, Graham."

"It shall be required, I am afraid," he replied clearing his throat.

An hour passed, as Graham and Julia ate their breakfast in silence. Ada came to retrieve their plates and gave a pleasant smile to Julia as she stood to leave the table. Julia returned a small smile and nodded her head.

She left the couple without a reply.

Julia stood beside Graham and reached for his hand. They walked together to the stairway leading to the second story wing where his father was living. The hallway was dim with only the light of one small candle lighting the way Graham held in his left hand, while his right hand led Julia behind him.

She followed him to the chamber wearing a mask of dread on her face. The dark fabric overhanging the large bed made a fearsome background giving pause to her footsteps as she entered. Graham continued to walk in the direction of the bed, then she followed, as a figure watched them enter, with a hostile expression. The pale face was pinched with a streak of perspiration across his forehead falling down to dark sunken eyes.

After a few moments, Graham walked closer to Edwina's side and gave her a look pleading for her to leave the chambers. She stood but hesitated in making a departure turning back to the ghastly figure lying in the bed. She sat back down beside the bed determined to remain at her post.

Julia turned her eyes from the man with a shameful dread at what was once a man who had the hearts of two women. She felt Edwina's hope for a moment of fear to seal her fate to leave Clark place, but she would fight through it.

Julia's chest tightened. This was the macabre meeting she had asked for but was now dreading. She had spent many long hours of the day hearing sounds in the mansion and wondering if it was Sir George Clark. She struggled daily to live in the bleak, crumbling mansion. Only Graham's warm love at night and Mary's good food and the conversation kept her from running back to her parents.

Graham gripped her hand tighter as they neared his father's bed together. Edwina stood up again and walked to the doorway to the left holding a large lantern. The drapes were heavy and black. They were pulled close to inhibit a drop of daylight from making an entrance.

Julia's eyes dropped to Sir George Clark's hands and she gasped. He was shackled from wrist to bed frame, with another chain holding his ankles to the bedposts of the footboard. She wanted to plead for him to be released, but she covered her mouth to remain silent.

Graham looked at Julia's reaction and watched her skin go pale. A streak of pain shot through his spine. Why did he allow his wife to see this?

Julia could not take her eyes off of the skinny old man. He was tiny, with a mass of wrangled white hair on his head. His mouth hung open preparing to speak.

"Stop right where you are," the old man commanded loudly.

"Let's stop here," whispered Graham.

"Why?" asked Edwina with a smile on her face.

"I have something in this bed with me and I am sure she does not want to inhale it," he said squirming in the bed. He nodded in Edwina's direction as she returned the nod and winked approval. "Graham, my son."

"Yes, father," said Graham releasing Julia's hand to hold her closer around the waist. "This is Julia, my wife. This is my father, Sir George Clark."

The chains clanked against the bedposts. "I am no Sir, right Missy? Tell, your wife to leave. Dear, this is no place for a beauty like you. I will treasure the sight of you though as I have been when I follow you around."

Julia stepped back remembering all of the eerie sounds she heard during her days in Clark Mansion. Graham pulled her closer to his side.

"We have come to see you, father. We have wonderful plans for Clark Mansion."

"That's enough! I do not want to hear of any of your foolish plans. I plan for it to crumble to dust along with all of my other plans. Those women keep haunting me and leave me no peace. Now move along, Graham, and release me from these chains Edwina," Sir George waved his hand in the direction of Graham and Julia.

Graham hugged Julia tightly. "No, father. You will talk to us in this manner. I will not have you disrespect my wife."

"Graham, no," said Julia softly. "We will follow the path of faith, not strife."

Graham coughed and released his arm from Julia's waist. He looked down at her and then turned toward his father, staring for a few moments longer.

As he walked over to his bedside, a lone tear fell from her eye, when she felt the soft touch of a hand on her arm. She turned to see Mary. Her smiling blue eyes looked happy, yet in pain. Julia breathed sensing her pulsating heartbeat calm down. Graham was here and Ada was here because she was here. Their joint compromise was grounded in love.

They stood at the foot of his bed looking down at the frail old man, as an eerie silence filled the room. Her stomach tightened into a knot while each clang of the shackles made her jump from foot to foot.

"Why are *you* here?" asked Sir George looking at Ada.

"I am here to support my...sister-in-law," she said throwing her shoulders back and looking Sir George in the eyes.

"Your *sister-in-law*? Not at all. You'll get not one shilling from me. Your mother took all of my dreams away with her. There is nothing left for you here, girl," said Sir George turning his head away from her.

Ada continued to look at him shaking her head from side to side.

"There is plenty here for her. There is plenty for all of us. I want to talk to you gentleman to gentleman, not as a shackled crazed shell of a man you once were," said Graham.

"What are you doing Dr. Graham?" asked Edwina stepping away from the wall.

"I am relieving you of your chains. You will be free to act and if it is disorderly, you shall pay the consequences. I have all respect for you as my father, but I will not hesitate to protect what is mine," said Graham looking over at Julia and Ada standing locked arm in arm.

Lightning cracked and both women recoiled in fright. They all soon heard the steady drops of rain on the rooftop.

"You did this, New Bride." Sir George narrowed his eyes on Julia. "You have killed my old son and now you bring this weakling to me."

Graham pressed his lips together as he removed the chains from his father's dirty ankles and wrists. The man shot up in the bed, grabbing the faded duvet to cover himself, then leaned back against the headboard with a smirk on his wrinkled face.

"We are not going to keep living in your dungeon, father. You have made one for us all, but I choose this day to shut it down. My bride and I are determined to make Clark Mansion a place of healing and love. With Julia and my sister Ada as support, I will become the physician my mother would be proud of. Do you want to join this mission or would you prefer to go elsewhere?"

Julia held her breath. The way Graham asked the question made her believe he knew the forthcoming answer. Sir George Clark frowned and buried his head in the duvet like a child receiving a harsh punishment. Edwina froze her hardened eyes on all three of them.

"Why are you putting your feeble father through this?" she asked her face flushing red. "For this poor lass?"

Ignoring her question, Graham turned to his father. "I know you and Edwina will not be pleased. She has tried to step in to support you in your madness after losing Ella, but I am stepping in now. I will begin to have my own family and I will not raise my children in darkness. There will be adequate light for all of us to flourish."

"You have lost all of your marbles, boy."

"Thank you, father. I lost them to fall in love with Julia and the possibility of a new and better life ahead. We will open a wing of this vast estate to operate as a hospital for the new year. A facility to treat the poor and sickly," said Graham smiling.

"That is a preposterous idea if I have ever heard of one," said Sir George lifting his head from the duvet.

Edwina stared at Graham with a quizzical look on her face. "Have you gone mad, Doctor?"

"No, but I am dismayed I let this go on far too long. No more, Edwina. Either you join us or you are free to leave with my father if he so chooses," Graham said his eyes glazing over.

Sir George could barely remain in the bed. She heard the bed frame rattle violently as his body filled with rage. His hands closed into fists pounding the feather mattress on both sides of him. "We have nowhere to go, boy."

"Then join us because I'm afraid wartime is finally over. Love shall reign here. I will see that Edwina continues to take care of you here. You can continue to live in the darkness of your room, but as for the rest of my estate, there shall be light," he stepped over to Julia and Ada and held out both hands while the two young women took hold of his hands.

"What are you going to do now?" asked Edwina her eyes wide.

'I'm going to prepare to celebrate Christmas and create a promising project. I have a wife and a sister that I am ready to build a new life with."

Julia and Ada smiled as they both began to cry. The three of them left the room together, hand in hand. Ada began to laugh through her tears as they made their way down the hallway.

"What are you laughing about Ada?" asked Julia.

She looked at Julia as she began smiling. "I bet Sir George never thought his madness would rub off on his family in this manner."

They all laughed at the top of the staircase.

"I am off to gather some holly and gather more candles for some decorations. Loads of festivities to prepare for now," said Ada as she bounded down the stairs leaving Julia and Graham alone.

"Oh my, what have I started?" laughed Graham.

"I cannot wait to see what shall become of us," replied Julia blinking back tears.

He chuckled and wiped the tears from her cheeks. "Me too."

Graham took Julia into his arms and kissed her fully. He was meeting himself in her and he liked what he saw. He understood the man he was before was not as broken as he believed. He had given the remedy to save her mother's life and she became the remedy to save his own.

As they broke their kiss, the rain came to a halt. The storm was over. Their love shining bright for each other for as long as they lived.

THE END

Thank you for taking the time out of your day to read *A Daughter's Christmas Hope* and spend the time to get to know my characters and this interesting place.

Find more titles by Lana Nolan on Amazon:

US │ UK │ CAN │ AUS

Feel free to contact Lana on Facebook.

Click here for New Book Release Notifications!

Keep reading to take a sneak peek at another story, *The Orphan's Family*.

Preview Look

Prologue

June 1840, London, England

Dean Edwin Nelson sat in his library, dressed for bed. He was fifty years old with a thin frame and a lean jawline. He wore a determined look as his gray eyes were always probing for answers.

The room he was sitting in had tall bookcases consumed with books. He was seated at a desk, looking over research papers as he sipped a glass of brandy. Every so often he would take a pensive glance out of the long window stretching as wide as the bookcases. The heavy drapes were pulled back to reveal a purple sky fading into the horizon.

Dean Nelson spun around in his chair as the door of his library flew open. His wife, Mrs. Jane Nelson, walked into the room rubbing her hands together. She was a finely built lady of forty-five years. Her green eyes had a touch of crimson red and her mouth was in a concrete frown.

She bent low to Dean Nelson, "She is not doing any better."

"Oh my dear, not the news I was expecting to hear," he said pulling his nightgown closer.

"There is a frosty chill this evening. The crisp air will not do her any good. Can you request more firewood be brought in for the fireplaces?"

"It will cost me more to keep this house heated. Do you think it is necessary to begin gathering more?" asked Dean Nelson.

"We want her to have the best chance for recovery," she replied.

"All right, have Franklin gather more wood to chop for the fireplaces. Then, after you have spoken to him, instruct young Emory to come and see me," said Dean Nelson.

Mrs. Nelson patted his shoulder, then walked out of the library and closed the door.

The Nelsons lived in a spacious well-built estate on the grounds of Kensingdale College. He had overseen the building of the structure. The brick home looked out over a rolling meadow.

Dean Nelson aspired to be a rich man and was raising his new family on the college grounds. He and Mrs. Nelson had taken in a lovely young girl, Elaina Nelson. She was seven years old. They also had her twelve-year-old brother named Emory Nelson.

He was a boy who enjoyed amusing himself. He was also a curious lad. If he was bored, there was always some type of mischief to be discovered, bringing his new father much dismay and resorting to his use of the leather strap. The boy was a thin child, from his days begging on the street for food, so Dean Nelson was often reluctant to take the strap but felt it necessary to show him a proper upbringing.

He had curly ash brown hair and had a sharp jawline similar to his new father. Whenever he did something to bring on the wrath of his father, he took it with a steady resolve. He never tried to run away like most children they had tried to take in before.

Elaina Nelson loved being with her older brother because he taught her games learned from the older children they spent time with on the streets. They walked the grounds of the college campus inspecting various locations and talking to anyone who crossed their path. Mrs. Nelson was often searching for a new governess to oversee her roving children. Many of the previous ones could never keep up with the adventurous pair.

Being a known animal lover on the campus, Mrs. Nelson had taken in a stray kitten. Dean Nelson was reluctant but allowed the small gray puffball to take refuge in their home after realizing it could keep the critters away. One morning, a month after the cat had made the Nelson home his own, he disappeared. Mrs. Nelson had the children look all over the campus for the cat.

Emory was able to bring in some burnt gray fur he had found. "I found it in the rubbish of the servants outside."

Mrs. Nelson sobbed uncontrollably and left the room.

Earlier in the day, Dean Nelson had walked home from class. As he neared his home, he glanced out in the meadow and saw his children playing. Elaina had a dark object in her arms while Emory held a stick in his hands.

Dean Nelson stopped walking and watched as Emory laid the stick on the object in Elaina's arms, and suddenly Elaina fell to the ground as the object tumbled out of her arms. Emory threw the stick on the object, then bent his legs to get on his knees. Dean Nelson became concerned and called their names. Emory hopped up and pulled Elaina to her feet. He ran to his father leaving Elaina straggling behind.

"We were pretending to be the characters in a book we read," said Emory when he reached his father.

"You left your sister. Are you certain, she is all right?" asked Dean Nelson.

"Yes, father," said Emory watching his sister struggle to walk towards them.

"Elaina, are you still pretending?" asked Dean Nelson as Elaina came closer. He walked over and picked her up. "Where is the toy you were holding?"

Elaina motioned to Emory with a puzzled look. Their father looked at Emory too. His face flushed red as he turned to run towards the house. Elaina lay her head on her father's shoulder as he carried her to the house.

Later that night, as Mrs. Nelson put the children to bed, she noticed Elaina's forehead was wet and warm. Still dealing with the grief of losing her cat, she dismissed it as simply playing in the evening air without the proper attire. She kissed her forehead and bid her a good slumber.

During the night, the child ran into her parent's bedchambers screaming for help. She leaped into the bed with trembling. She held on to her mother and kept repeating, "Don't let them get me. Don't let them get me."

She did not fall asleep until the early morning. The servants moved the little girl's belongings to another bedchamber. Elaina's skin had turned pale and clammy. Throughout the day, she did not have the strength to eat or leave the bed. Dean Nelson called for the closest doctor who gave the parents a grim prognosis of Diphtheria for little Elaina.

Dean Nelson called Emory to his library.

"Why do you think your little sister is ill, son?"

"I have no idea, father," replied Emory.

"She seemed fine up until you were both playing in the meadow."

"I passed along some stories to her and Elaina became frightened."

"What kind of stories?"

"Some old woman passing through campus told me the stories. I added more to the stories and we acted some of them out."

"Young man, I have told you to stop meddling in other people's affairs and not to talk to everyone who crosses your path."

"I know father, but I am bored throughout the day and love hearing interesting tales."

"You should take more interest in your studies young man," said Dean Nelson in a stern tone.

"Yes, sir," said Emory lowering his eyes. "Father, I still do not understand how old stories could make Elaina sick?"

"That is *the* mystery, Emory. What about the stick you placed on the object she was holding?"

Emory looked at his father wide-eyed.

"Do you recall the precise moment, son?"

"Yes, it was of no importance. We were playing Father."

"Well, Emory, it is of importance to poor Elaina at this time," said Dean Nelson.

Emory lowered his head and stared at the floor.

"You are a child and I do not lay blame on you, but your game may not be as innocent as you believe," said Dean Nelson sitting back in his chair.

They both looked up as Mrs. Nelson burst through the door with tears in her eyes.

"I believe we are losing her."

"No, do not say such words," said Dean Nelson as he jumped from the chair and dashed out of the room following Mrs. Nelson.

Emory stood rooted in the same spot and sobbed.

A half-hour later, a servant retrieved the boy from his father's library to speak with his parents.

Mrs. Nelson came out of Elaina's bedchambers, wiping tears from her face. "Go in and speak to your sister, Emory," said Mrs. Nelson. "I am sure it would please her."

He struggled to speak. "I cannot...do not ask...me...to go in there," pleaded the boy.

"Yes, you can and you should. She is your only sister."

"I don't want to see her in that state. I want to remember her being happy, not cold and in a dark place."

"What dark place?" asked Mrs. Nelson.

"Maybe, I put her in that place."

Dean Nelson walked out of Elaina's bedroom.

His wife looked over at him. "I do not understand him. What is Emory talking about?"

"She is such great pain, I fear we may be losing her," said Dean Nelson tears streaming down his face. He hugged his wife and they clung to each other as they grieved.

He reached for his son, but the boy stood back in the shadows of the dim hallway. The Nelsons walked back in Elaina's room together to grieve at her bedside.

Elaina Nelson was buried at the campus chapel yard. The family attempted to continue with their daily life, but her early death ruled their daily thoughts. Dean Nelson could not forget about the spectacle of his daughter falling on the ground that day. He could not bury the words his son told him about an old woman and her stories. However, he did not bring it up with Emory as he could not bear to speak about the bizarre sight again.

One cold and blistering evening, Dean Nelson was walking home and ran into his son outside of their residence. He was staring off at the meadow that he and Elaina once played in. He grabbed his son and held him close.

"Will you tell me one day what you did, son?" Dean Nelson whispered in Emory's ear.

The boy broke his father's embrace and backed away. His face ashen white, he turned and ran from the house. His father watched him run and felt the impulse to call for his return but remained mute in a grief-stricken state.

Later that evening, Dean Nelson sent a group of servants out to search for Emory after he failed to return home for dinner. The wind blew cold throughout the night with no sight or sound of the boy's whereabouts. The Nelsons did not sleep that night awaiting word from anyone about their son.

The next morning, a groundskeeper paid a visit to the Nelson residence with news he had located their son. The Dean and the groundskeeper raced out of the home. The groundskeeper led him to the fresh burial site of Elaina to find Emory's frail body spread across her grave face down in the dirt. His clothes were mudstreaked and his face blistered by the cold wind.

Emory whispered with his eyes closed, "Lay me to rest beside my sister."

His father shook his head in disbelief as the servants carried him away from the grounds of the chapel.

You can find *The Orphan's Family* on Amazon.

About the Author

Lana Nolan has always been interested in the lives of those who lived centuries ago and the history behind the drama of their existence. She spends her free time visiting museums and watching documentaries learning about the past to inspire new stories for her books.

Printed in Great Britain
by Amazon